The Berenstain Bears'
TROUBLE WITH PETS

Cubs don't expect
the big job they will get
when they jump up and down
and beg for a pet.

A First Time Book®

The Berenstain Bears

Random House 🏠 New York

Copyright © 1990 by Berenstains, Inc. All rights reserved under International and Pan-American Copyright Conventions. Published in the United States by Random House, Inc., New York, and simultaneously in Canada by Random House of Canada Limited, Toronto.

Library of Congress Cataloging-in-Publication Data:
Berenstain, Stan.   The Berenstain Bears' trouble with pets / Stan & Jan Berenstain.   p.   cm. — (A First time book) SUMMARY: Brother and Sister Bear learn that a new puppy is not a plaything, but a responsibility.   ISBN 0-679-80848-5 (pbk.) : — ISBN 0-679-90848-X (lib. bdg.)   [1. Pets—Fiction. 2. Dogs—Fiction. 3. Bears—Fiction.] I. Berenstain, Jan. II. Title. III. Series: Berenstain, Stan. First time books. PZ7.B4483Bfq 1990 [E]—dc20 90-32956 CIP   AC

Manufactured in the United States of America   15   16   17

TROUBLE WITH PETS

Stan & Jan Berenstain

"Good-bye, Little Bird," said Sister Bear. "Fly away and be happy." On her finger was the sparrow that the Bear family had taken in because it had an injured leg. Papa Bear had made a splint for it out of a toothpick and strips of tape.

Brother and Sister had named it
[Tw]eetie and had taken care of it
[fo]r about a week. But now it was
[ti]me to remove the splint and let
[th]e bird go back to nature, where
[it] belonged. It hopped
[o]nto a twig, then
[to]ok wing.

Before you could
say "Tweetie," it was
out of sight.

"I'm going to miss our little bird," said Sister, sadly. "Tweetie was such a nice little pet."

"Tweetie wasn't a pet, dear," said Mama Bear, "not a real pet, anyway. It was an injured bird that we helped get well so it could go back to the forest."

"Why don't we get a real pet, Mama?" asked Sister.

"Other cubs have pets," said Brother. "Why can't we? Cousin Freddy has a dog. Lizzy Bruin has a cat. Too-Tall Grizzly has a snake."

"Well," said Mama as they climbed the front steps of the tree house, "I suppose it's something to think about."

"Gee, Mama," said Brother. "What's there to think about?"

"There's quite a lot to think about," she said. "A pet is a big responsibility. A pet has to be fed, cared for, kept clean—what do you think, Papa?"

"I think a dog would be nice," said Papa.

"But a dog is an *especially* big responsibility," protested Mama. "A dog needs shots. It needs to be trained and walked—and there are dog laws..."

"A big dog," said Papa, "about so high, that can go fetch and play Frisbee..."

"We'll take care of it, Mama!" cried the cubs. "We promise! We promise!"

"Remember now," said Mama as they piled into the car, "we're going to the pet shop just to look. Choosing a pet—especially a dog—is serious business."

"Speaking of dogs," said Papa, pointing to a sign as they drove by Farmer Ben's place.

"'Puppies Available—See Farmer Ben,'" said Brother, reading the sign aloud. "How about that? Ben's dog, Bess, must have had pups!"

"May we look at them, Mama?" cried Sister. "Oh, please, Mama, please!"

Before Mama could answer, Papa said, "No harm in looking," and pulled into Farmer Ben's driveway.

Ben's dog, Bess, had indeed had pups: five of the cutest, roly-poliest little balls of fur you've ever seen.

Farmer Ben picked one up and put it in Sister's arms.

"What beautiful brown eyes!" she said. "May we have this one, Mama? May we? May we? Please!"

"Most pups have brown eyes," said Ben. "But I do think that one is the pick of the litter. It's yours if you like—a gift from Bess and me."

"Goodness," said Mama. "That's very generous of you, Ben. I really don't know what to say."

"'Yes!' Say 'yes!'" shouted the cubs, jumping up and down.

"It certainly is a cute little thing," she said. "All right, then—yes."

Brother and Sister were overjoyed. "Thank you! Thank you, Farmer Ben!" they shouted. Then, after they had calmed down a bit, Brother said, "Hmm...Our pup's going to need a name—how about King, or Prince, or maybe Duke?"

Farmer Ben, who was an expert in such matters, took a quick look under the pup's tail and said, "The only trouble with those names, Brother Bear, is that this pup is a girl."

Of course, they couldn't take their new pet home with them. It would need its mother's milk for a couple more weeks. But there was plenty of puppy talk as they headed home: talk about names, talk about where the puppy would sleep, and talk about who would take care of it.

"Remember now," said
Mama. "You've promised to
take care of the new pup: to
feed and water it, and to
clean up after it when it
has accidents."

"What kind of accidents?"
asked Sister.

"We'll discuss that
later," Mama said.

Brother and Sister couldn't believe how lucky they'd been. A new puppy, for their very own! That night, before falling asleep, they thought about some of the wonderful things they would do with their new pet.

Sister thought about dressing it in doll's clothes and pushing it in her doll carriage.

She thought about introducing it to her stuffed toys. Perhaps they could have a tea party.

Brother's thoughts were quite different; he thought about winning the blue ribbon at the Bear Country Dog Show.

He thought how fine it would be to shout "Mush!" as his great dog pulled him through the deep snow.

But, of course, a puppy isn't a toy to be dressed in doll's clothes. It's a living creature with a mind and nature of its own.

It would be a long time before the pup could compete for blue ribbons. It would be an even longer time before it could pull anything through the snow.

There was no question about
Brother and Sister had a lot to
learn about puppies. So Mama
Papa decided that a trip to the
library was in order. They took
out a book called *Puppy Care*.

When the big day came, the Bear
family had a puppy-care plan all
worked out. First, they stopped
off at the police station to get
her registered.

"What's the little lady's name?" asked Officer Marguerite. The pup would need a license with her name and address on it in case she got lost. But Brother and Sister still hadn't agreed on a name. What to do?

"It seems to me that Officer Marguerite just named our pup," said Mama. "Little Lady sounds like an excellent name to me." So the puppy left the police station with a name as well as a license.

Next, a quick stop at the pet shop for a puppy harness and leash, then a very important stop at the vet's for a checkup and shots. Little Lady didn't like the shots one bit. Brother and Sister knew just how she felt. They even sort of knew how parents must feel when their cubs have to get shots.

DOCTOR
OF
VETERINARY
MEDICINE

Now it was time to introduce Little Lady to her new home. The Bears had already gotten food for her and had made a puppy box out of a cardboard carton and an old blanket. They had placed the box in the kitchen, where it was nice and warm— with the door closed, of course. Puppies tend to get into mischief, and there wasn't much harm she could do in the kitchen.

Little Lady sniffed all around the kitchen, then curled up in her box and went to sleep.

At first, the cubs argued about whose turn it was to feed, water, and walk the pup.

IT'S <u>MY</u> TURN!

NO, IT'S <u>MY</u> TURN!

But after a while they began to argue about whose turn it *wasn't*.

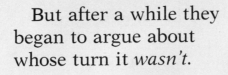

IT'S <u>YOUR</u> TURN. I CLEANED UP AFTER THE LAST ACCIDENT!

NO, IT'S YOUR TURN! <u>I</u> CLEANED UP AFTER THE LAST ACCIDENT!

Mama solved that problem by posting a puppy-care schedule on the wall.

PY CARE
DULE
ON: SIS
ES: BRO
ED: SIS
P THURS: BRO
CLEAN-UP FRI: SIS
T: BRO

Not that the puppy was all work and
no fun. Little Lady was, indeed, a lot of
fun. In fact, it was so much fun watching
her that the Bear family didn't watch
much television anymore.

She chased her tail.

She did somersaults.

She "fought" her
rubber dog bone.

And she got into the strangest positions.

Also, of course, she grew. She grew so much that the Bear family started calling her Lady instead of Little Lady. And, like all puppies, she loved to chew.

Then one day somebody forgot to close the kitchen door while the family went shopping. When they got back, they found that Lady had chewed up half the living room.

The time had come for Lady
to have her own house out in
the yard. Papa built a fine,
sturdy doghouse.

Then he chicken-wired
the fence to keep her
safely in the yard.

Lady loved her house.

She was even more fun in the yard than she was in the house. She chased leaves in the fall,

snowflakes in the winter,

cherry blossoms in the spring,

and butterflies in the summer.

And as the years went by, Lady became more than a pet. She became another member of the family, to love and enjoy.